Jelly Beans

The really, really, really big dinosaur

Richard Byrne

OXFORD
UNIVERSITY PRESS

'One for him and one for me.

One for him and one for me.'

Finlay was sharing out jelly beans
to have with his friend when . . .

a **big dinosaur** walked past.

'Would you like a jelly bean?'
asked Finlay.

'I want them all!'
said the big (and rather rude) dinosaur.

'Oh, I couldn't give them
all to you,' said Finlay,
'you see, they belong
to my friend.'

'Well tell your little friend, wherever he is, that I want **his jelly beans!**'

'He's asleep,' said Finlay. 'But he's a really, really, really **big** friend.'

'Oh, I'm really, **really, really** scared!' said the big (and rather cheeky) dinosaur. 'Everyone knows I'm the **biggest** and **strongest** dinosaur around here! Just w-a-i-t and . . .

(and rather heavy) rock up the hill towards Finlay.

'You'll have to do better than that,' said Finlay bravely.

'Everyone knows my friend can eat show-offs like you for breakfast.'

'You're making
that up,'
said the big dinosaur.
'Anyway, I'm
definitely the best at jumping

'Well I'd like to see your pretend friend

the JELLY BEANS!'

'You can shout as much as you like,' said Finlay, 'but my friend can shout louder.'

'Look here, **tinysaur**, what **can't** this make-believe friend of yours do?'

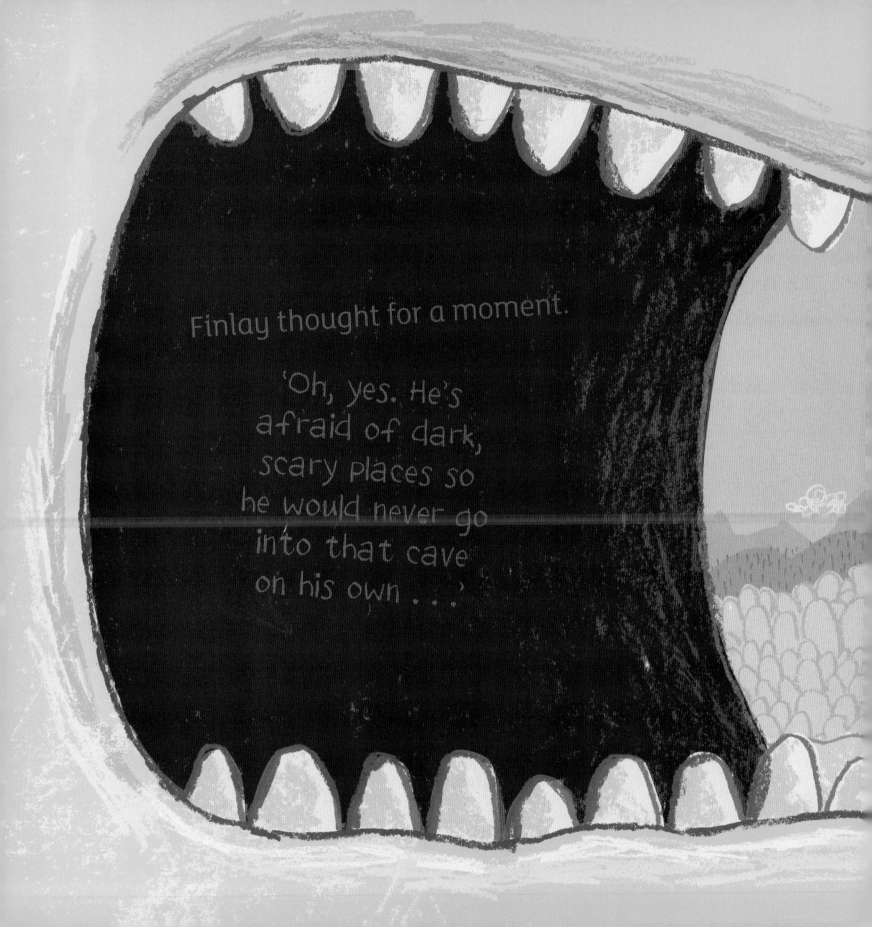

Finlay thought for a moment.

'Oh, yes. He's afraid of dark, scary places so he would never go into that cave on his own . . .'

Just then, the big dinosaur grabbed
the jar of jelly beans and ran into the cave.

Finlay giggled. 'Don't worry, he **could** eat you but he **won't**!'

'**JELLY BEANS AND TREETOPS ARE MY FAVOURITES!**' said the really, really, really big (and rather friendly) dinosaur.

'I won't be a greedy show-off ever again!' promised the big dinosaur.

'First one to the bottom wins the jelly beans!' said Finlay playfully.

Everyone knew that the big dinosaur was the best at S-l-i-d-i-n-g.

But this time . . .

For Stella, Ellis, Harley, Archie, Kim, Mia and Ella.
And a really, really, really big thank you to Helen and Karen.

OXFORD
UNIVERSITY PRESS

Great Clarendon Street, Oxford OX2 6DP

Oxford University Press is a department of the University of Oxford.
It furthers the University's objective of excellence in research,
scholarship, and education by publishing worldwide in

Oxford   New York

Auckland Cape Town Dar es Salaam Hong Kong Karachi
Kuala Lumpur Madrid Melbourne Mexico City Nairobi
New Delhi Shanghai Taipei Toronto

With offices in
Argentina Austria Brazil Chile Czech Republic France Greece
Guatemala Hungary Italy Japan Poland Portugal Singapore
South Korea Switzerland Thailand Turkey Ukraine Vietnam

Oxford is a registered trade mark of Oxford University Press
in the UK and in certain other countries

Text and illustrations © Richard Byrne 2012

The moral rights of the author/illustrator have been asserted
Database right Oxford University Press (maker)

First published in 2012
This edition first published in 2019.

British Library Cataloguing in Publication Data
Data available

ISBN: 978-0-19-276886-5 (paperback)

10 9 8 7 6 5 4 3 2 1

Printed in China

Paper used in the production of this book is a natural,
recyclable product made from wood grown in sustainable forests.
The manufacturing process conforms to the environmental
regulations of the country of origin.

Ideas for when you're sharing
The Really, Really, Really, Really Big Dinosaur

What did dinosaurs really like to eat?

The answer to the following five questions is either 'Finlay' or 'the big dinosaur'.

Ready . . . ?

1. Who has a spike on his nose?
2. Who has just two teeth?
3. Who has floppy ears?
4. Who shows off?
5. Who is smarter?

This story is about sharing. When the big dinosaur learns to share, he discovers two good new friends. Apart from books (*obviously!*) what do you like to share?

Finlay is quite an unusual dinosaur as he likes to eat jelly beans! Can you name all the colours of the jelly beans that Finlay has in his jar?

Sometimes in the pictures there are very pale prehistoric fossils hidden in the background. See if you can spot them while you share the story. Some of them are quite tricky to find!

If you like counting, you could try counting the numbers of dinosaur teeth or dinosaur scales that you can see on each page.